My grandma and grandpa were always busy with their hobbies. Grandpa painted and Grandma loved making cakes.

One day, Grandma decided they should get outside and do more things together. "Mountain climbing," she suggested. "Good exercise and lots of fresh air."

Grandpa wasn't so sure.

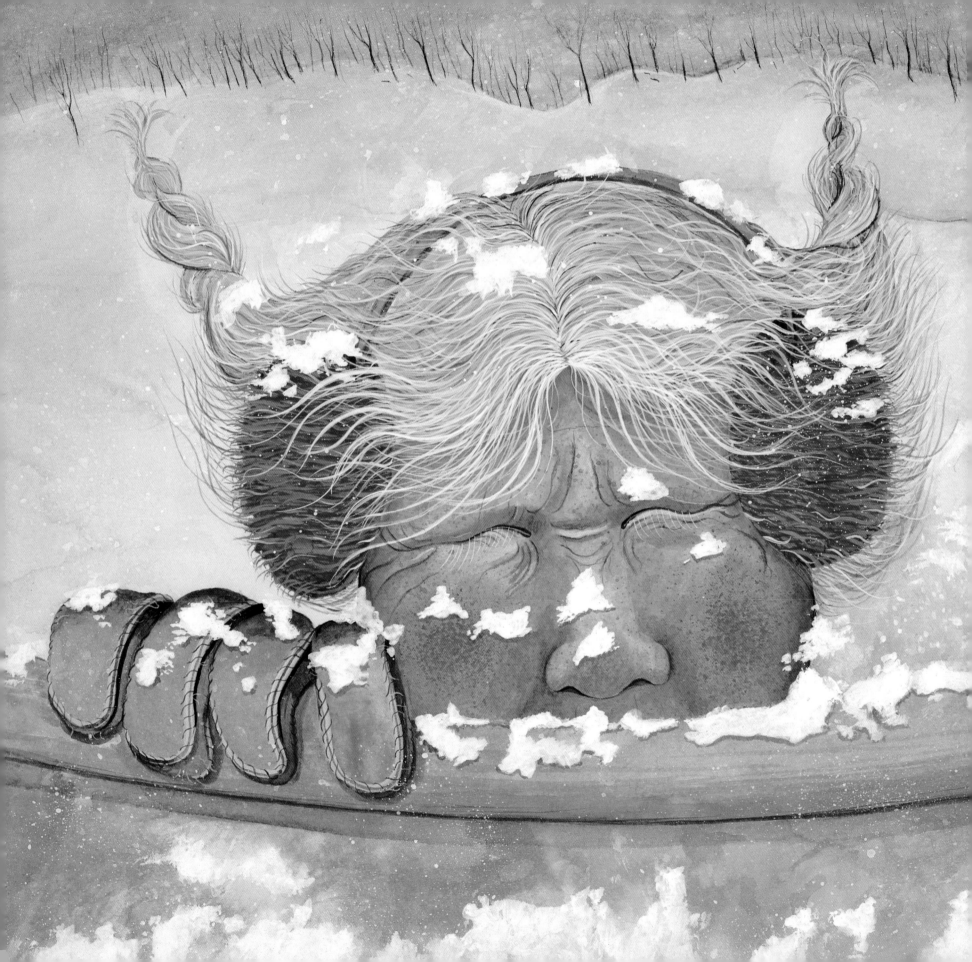

In the winter, Grandma took him sledding.

Spring brought lots of water down from the mountains.
"Perfect for canoeing," Grandma said.

Grandpa wasn't so sure about canoeing...

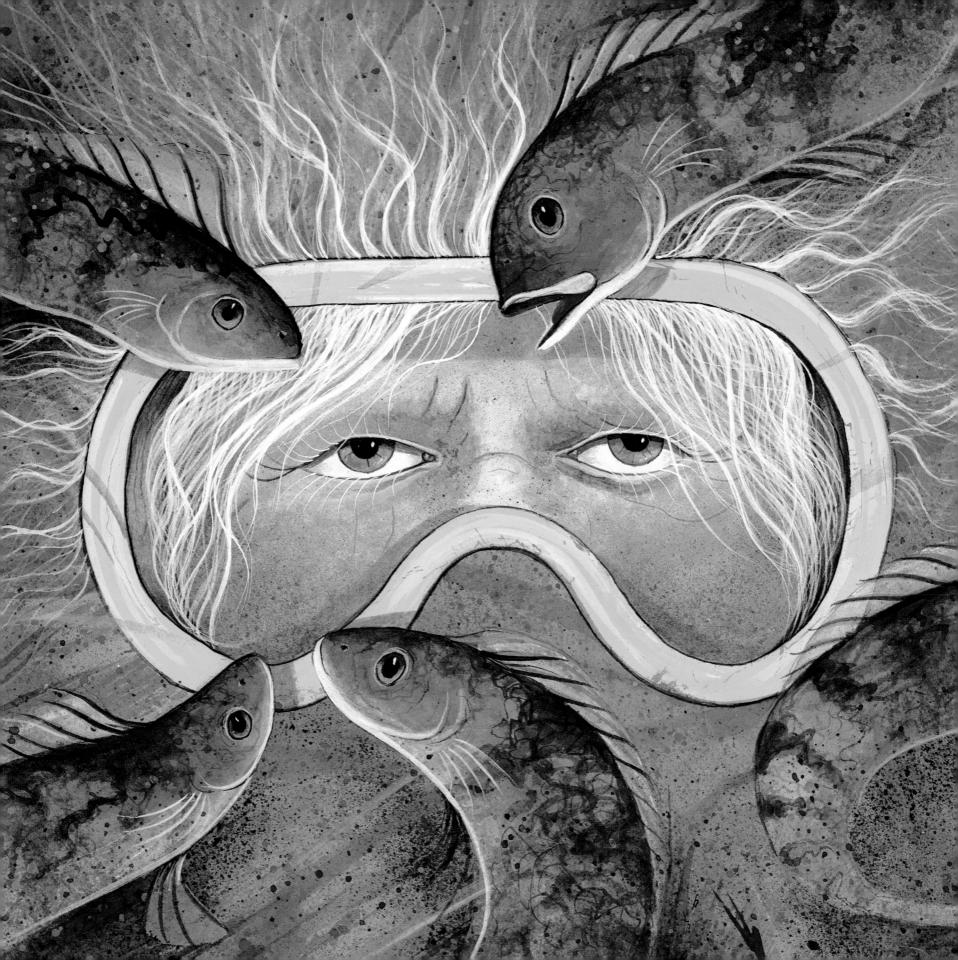

...or anything to do with water.

Summer seemed the perfect time to get out into the country, but Grandpa didn't agree.

When Grandma was young,
she loved to go horseback riding.
She thought Grandpa would enjoy it, too.

FOXTROT CHAMPIONS 1949
TROCODERO

I thought they
could try a little dancing—
they used to when they were younger.

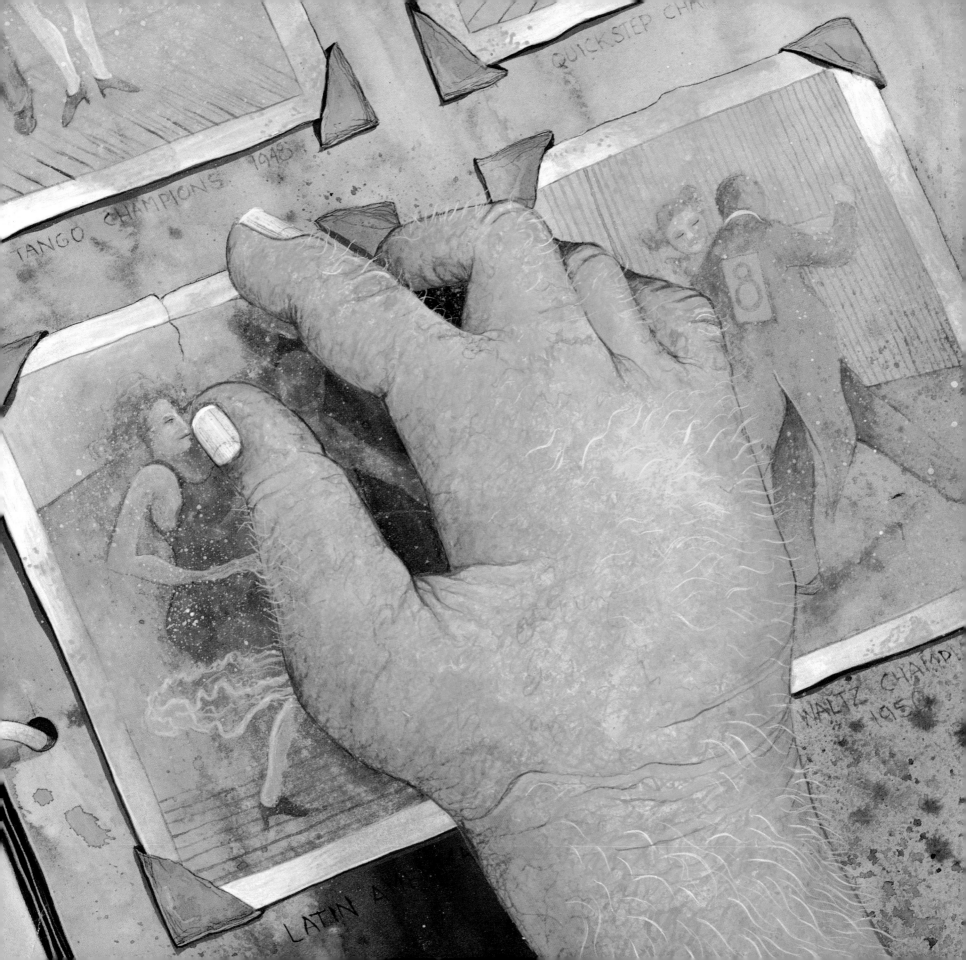

But modern dancing
was so fast and the music so loud
that Grandpa couldn't keep up with Grandma anymore.

"Sailing," Grandma said. She was sure Grandpa could manage that.

Grandpa didn't get any fun out of sailing...

...or exploring caves.

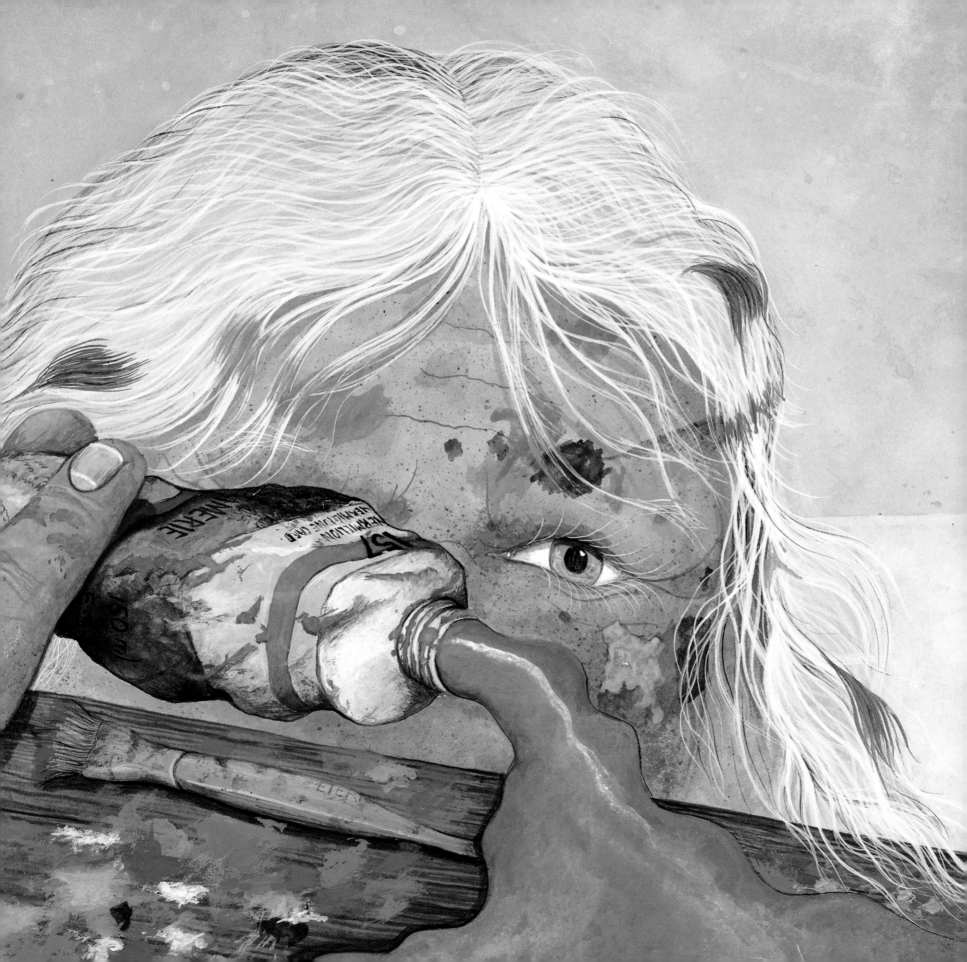

Feeling a little tired
from all the exercise,
Grandpa finally cried,
"Why can't we just
stay home?"

But home wasn't quite the same—
until I asked, "Why don't you do
what you used to do, just like before?"

And they did.